PEARL

PAINTS

Abigail Thomas

Illustrated by Margaret Hewitt

Henry Holt and Company · New York

Henry Holt and Company, Inc.
Publishers since 1866
115 West 18th Street
New York, New York 10011

Henry Holt is a registered
trademark of Henry Holt and Company, Inc.

Published in Canada by Fitzhenry & Whiteside Ltd.,
195 Allstate Parkway, Markham, Ontario L3R 4T8.

Library of Congress Cataloging-in-Publication Data
Thomas, Abigail. Pearl paints / Abigail Thomas;
illustrated by Margaret Hewitt.
Summary: Using her new set of watercolors,
Pearl paints a masterpiece.
[1. Artists—Fiction.   2. Painting—Fiction.]
I. Hewitt, Margaret, ill.   II. Title.
PZ7.T364Pe 1994   [E]—dc20   93-41368

ISBN 0-8050-2976-1
First Edition—1994
Printed in the United States of America
on acid-free paper. ∞

1 3 5 7 9 10 8 6 4 2

The artist used pastels, ink,
and gouache on printmaking paper to
create the illustrations for this book.

For my grandsons, Joe and Sam, and for Caitlin
—A. T.

For Mom
—M. H.

Pearl got a set of colors for her birthday. She got brushes and paper, too. And now Pearl paints. She paints and paints.

"Don't you want your lunch?" asks Pearl's mother. "Aren't you hungry?"

Pearl shakes her head. "No, thank you," she says. "I'm too busy." Pearl has a brushful of blue. Now a brushful of purple.

"What's that you're painting?" asks Pearl's mother.

"I don't know yet," says Pearl. She paints some stars. She paints a moon.

"Oh," says her mother. "I see."

Pearl paints more moons. Big fat moons, little skinny moons. Moons in all shapes and sizes.

"How come so many moons?" asks Pearl's brother, Willy.

"I like moons," says Pearl. She has a brushful of orange.

"Me too," says Willy. He watches Pearl paint. "Paint a horse," says Willy. "Paint me on it."

Pearl paints. She paints and paints.

"That's a cow," says Willy. "That's not a horse."

"I like cows," says Pearl.

"Don't put me on that cow," says Willy.

Pearl keeps painting.

"That's not me," says Willy. "That's not my hat."

"Come out and play," calls Pearl's friend Laura. "Come out and play with us."

"Can't," says Pearl. "I'm too busy."

"When will you be through?" asks Laura.

"I don't know," says Pearl. "After this, there might be another one."

"You can't just stand there and paint for the rest of your life," says Laura, stamping her foot. "You're a little girl!"

"I know that," says Pearl. "That's why I can't stop now."

"You have to go to school tomorrow," says Laura, and runs off to the swings.

Outside, the sun is going down. Pearl has a brushful of pink.

"It's time for supper," says Pearl's father.

Pearl eats with her left hand. She paints with her right. She paints in the air above the table. Pearl's hands are stained with color. Her hands are green and blue and red and orange.

"What are you making now?" asks Willy.

"I don't know yet," says Pearl. "I'm just imagining."

After supper, Pearl paints.

"What shall we do?" worries Pearl's mother.

"What shall we think?" worries Pearl's father.

"Let her be," says Pearl's aunt Peg. "Painters paint. That's what they do. Pearl's a painter, sure enough."

"She's running out of colors," says Willy. "She's almost out of blue. She's almost out of green."

"Time for bed," says Pearl's father.
"But I'm not finished," says Pearl.
"Time for bed anyway," says Pearl's mother.

In her dreams, Pearl paints. She paints the whole sky;
she paints the trees.

She paints the oceans and the ocean depths with all the fishes and all the whales.

She paints the jungles, and the forests, . . .

. . . and the desert sands, which shift and shift again. She paints the camels. She paints the cactuses. She paints the birds in the air and the worms in the ground.

Then she wakes up. It is a school day.

Pearl is in class. She looks out the window. She is thinking about painting.

"Wake up," says Miss Featherton.

"I am awake," says Pearl.

"What is twelve times twelve?" asks Miss Featherton.
"Reddish brown," says Pearl. "With a little gray." She
has been thinking of a certain kind of squirrel.

"No more art for a while," says Pearl's mother, reading the note from school. "Homework comes first."

Pearl has a hard time concentrating on arithmetic. She has a hard time with her spelling words. Everything reminds Pearl of painting.

"Spell *ocean*," says Pearl's mother. "Spell *meadow*. Spell *mountain, parrot, elephant*."

Finally, Pearl's homework is finished. And so Pearl paints. She paints and paints. She paints everything in the world she can think of . . . and even some things she can't.

In the morning, Pearl has no colors left. Every jar is empty. No more red or orange or green or blue. No more yellow. No more pink or black or purple. No more brown or silver. No more white. But what a picture she has painted.

mural by Pearl

Word travels fast.

"Oh my, oh my," says Pearl's mother and father.

"That's my girl," says Aunt Peg.

"That's me," says Willy, "under the sombrero."
"Paint me something," say all Pearl's friends.
"Paint me something," says Miss Featherton.
Pearl is proud, and everyone is proud of Pearl.

And best of all, they all brought Pearl paint!